A Picnic with Friends

Rebecca Irvin Clement

Picnic Time

Rebecca Clement
Copyright 2003

It's pic-nic time, pic-nic time. All our friends are here. Winter's gone. Snow melts a-way.

Spring is in the air. Please join us, birds. Squirrels come, too. We have stories to share.

Sun stays long. Birds sing a song. Spring is in the air.

"It's spring.
Time for a Bear Family picnic,"
said Bonnie.

"Let's ask our friends to go on our picnic," said Little Billy Bear.

"Friends are nice," said Bonnie Bear. "I'll ask our friends." And she did.

"No, thank you," said the goat. "I have to chew, chew, chew."

8

"Duck, Duck," said Bonnie, "will you come to our picnic?"

"Jay, Jay,"
said Bonnie, "will you come
to our picnic?"

"Squirrel, Squirrel," said Bonnie, "will you come to our picnic?"

"YES! Thank you,"
said the squirrel. "I will bring
my friend." And he DID!

Get the Animal Facts

Goats
Oberhasli goats are dairy goats from Switzerland. Their milk is good to drink and cheese made from the milk is good to eat. They eat grass, hay, oats and tree bark. The male is called a buck or billy, the female is called a doe or nanny and the babies are called kids.

Ducks
Mallard ducks live in ponds, lakes and rivers. They eat grasses, weeds and insects. The male is called a drake and has a bright green head. The female is brown and is called a hen. She lays ten to twelve eggs in her nest and sits on them for 28 days before they hatch into little ducklings.

Squirrels
Arctic ground squirrels live in groups or colonies of hundreds of squirrels. They live in burrows under the ground. They hibernate in the winter. They eat seeds, berries, willows, leaves, grasses and flowers.

Rabbits
Dutch lop-eared rabbits can be good pets for kids. They eat grasses and plants. The female rabbit is called a doe and her babies are called kittens. The male is called a buck.

Steller's Jay
The Steller's jay is found in forests in Alaska and the western United States, Canada, Mexico and Central America. It eats seeds, berries, nuts and insects. Jays are related to crows, ravens and magpies. They are believed to be the smartest of all the birds.

For more information and links see our web site: www.alaskaadventurebears.com

Meet the Alaska Adventure Bears

Bonnie, Bob and Little Billy love the long summer days in Alaska. They like to go on picnics. Bob flies their airplane to favorite streams and they fish for salmon. Bonnie likes to pick berries and make jam. Little Billy likes to read and play hockey. He wants to fly jets when he grows up. In the winter they like to ride snowmachines to their cabin near Mt. McKinley.

Bonnie, Bob and Little Billy

Grizzly Girls

Grizzly Gail likes to look for sea stars and shells on the beach. She likes camping and sleeping in a tent with her cousins, Garbo and Grace. Gail takes piano lessons and gets good grades on her report card. She also likes to go to movies. Her favorite color is pink.

Grizzly Garbo is the oldest of the Grizzly Girls. She likes to be the boss and tell her cousins what to do when the family goes on an adventure. In the summer, Garbo plays soccer and in the winter she likes to snowboard. Her favorite color is green.

Grizzly Grace loves books about birds. She earned a bird-watching badge in Girl Scouts. She likes to draw, write stories and make clothes for her dolls. Her favorite color is red. She is afraid of spiders but not big bears.